PARTY!
THIS WAY

First edition for the United States and Canada published in 2016 by Barron's Educational Series, Inc.

Originally published in 2015 by Simon and Schuster UK Ltd
1st floor, 222 Gray's Inn Road
London, UK WC1X 8HB
A CBS Company

All inquiries should be addressed to:
Barron's Educational Series, Inc.
250 Wireless Boulevard
Hauppauge, NY 11788
www.barronseduc.com
ISBN: 978-1-4380-0824-0
Library of Congress Control Number: 2015957310
Date of Manufacture: March 2016
Manufactured by: Toppan Leefung Printing LTD., Dongguan, China
Printed in China
9 8 7 6 5 4 3 2 1

Visit www.carylhart.com and www.deborahallwright.com

there's a MONSTER in my fridge

CARYL HART
Deborah Allwright

BARRON'S

What's that hiding behind the door?
Its feet have **squelched** across the floor . . .

Take care! Don't look! It's vile and smelly.

M

What's that hiding behind the screen,
With a **pointy hat** and **skin of green?**

I'm much too scared to look.
Are you?

Below our stairs, it's **dark** and **cold.**

It's full of **spiders,** dust, and mold.

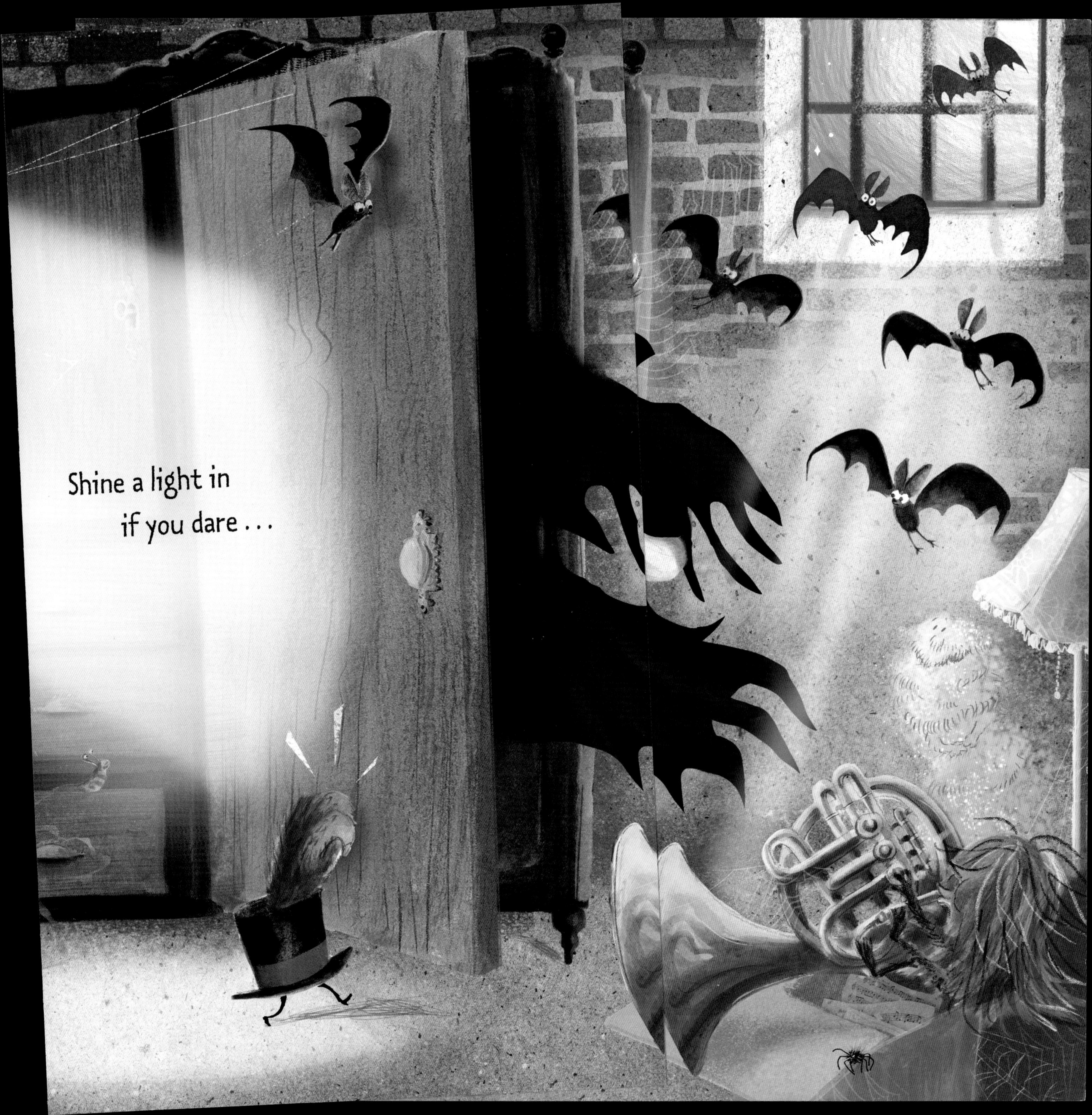

Shine a light in
if you dare . . .

What's that **splashing** in our bath?
It has a hollow, **rattly** laugh.

Take a peek.

Go on, be brave . . .

Tucked in bed, there's something **scary.**
Its fangs are **sharp,** its back is

HAIRY!

Lift the sheet. What will you find?

But look, what's this? A secret door!
A staircase to another floor.

Quiet as mice, don't dare to speak.
Slowly, lift the trap door . . .

CREAK!

Tiptoe carefully as can be, who's that hiding?